Rock Your Mocs

by Laurel Goodluck   illustrated by Madelyn Goodnight

Heartdrum

An Imprint of HarperCollinsPublishers

Pronunciation Guide

Characters and Words

Ajuawak	Ah-jew-WALK
Alyssa	ah-LIS-ah
Ellie	EL-lē
Forrest	FȮR-əst
Kalen	KĀ-lehn
kamipiak (plural for kamik)	KUHM-mee-pee-AHK
Kayla	KA-luh
Kyah	KĒ-ya
Kylie	KĪ-lē
Maria	Mä-RĒ-äh
Povi	PŌ-vē
Riley	RI-lee
Sa'ya (grandma)	sā-YAH
Taktuk	TUHK-TOOK
Tristen	TRIST-en

Names of Nations and Tribes

Colville	KOL-vil
Hidatsa	Hi-DÄT-sə
Hopi-Tewa	HŌ-pē
Inupiaq	i-NÜ- pē-‚ät
Little Shell Chippewa	CHI-pə-wä
Menominee	mə-NÄ-mə-nē
Navajo	NA-və-hō
Ojibwe	ō-JIB-wä
Osage	ō-SĀJ
Seminole	SE-mə-‚nōl
Tuscarora	tə-skə-RȮR-ə
Yurok	'YU-räk

Heartdrum is an imprint of HarperCollins Publishers. · Rock Your Mocs · Text copyright © 2023 by Laurel Goodluck · Illustrations copyright © 2023 by Madeline Goodnight
All rights reserved. Manufactured in Italy. · No part of this book may be used or reproduced in any manner whatsoever without written permission except in the case of brief quotations
embodied in critical articles and reviews. For information address HarperCollins Children's Books, a division of HarperCollins Publishers, 195 Broadway, New York, NY 10007.
www.harpercollinschildrens.com · Library of Congress Control Number: 2022930130 · ISBN 978-0-06-309989-0
Typography by Chelsea C. Donaldson · 23 24 25 26 27 RTLO 10 9 8 7 6 5 4 3 2 1 · First Edition

To all my great-nieces and great-nephews and
all children rockin' into the future!

—L.G.

To all the First American children who celebrate their
heritage every year, and to all of the artisans and moccasin-
makers who create these important pieces of culture

—M.G.

We're stepping out
and kicking it up.
It's a rockin' day.

Across Turtle Island and
across Indigenous Nations.
At schools, in cities and towns,
there's a celebration beginning.

We're stylin' today as we Rock Our Mocs!

We Rock Our Mocs
with pride!

Kyah strikes a pose
in her Yurok mocs.

Taktuk, who is Inupiaq,
slips on his kamipiak,

then gives his dad a high five.

We Rock Our Mocs
with style!

Alyssa's Colville beads
shimmer and shine
in her favorite colors.

Riley tips his Little Shell Chippewa swag.
Moccasins made with deer, elk, moose, or seal
and love, stories, and laughter.

With skilled hands and knowledge passed down,
moccasins are works of art we wear, so we Rock Our Mocs!

We Rock Our Mocs
because they are precious gifts!

As babies enter the world,
we are thankful.
Kalen curls his toes
in his first Navajo mocs.

Some mocs are passed down,
but Povi's Hopi-Tewa mocs
are traced to fit by my sa'ya.

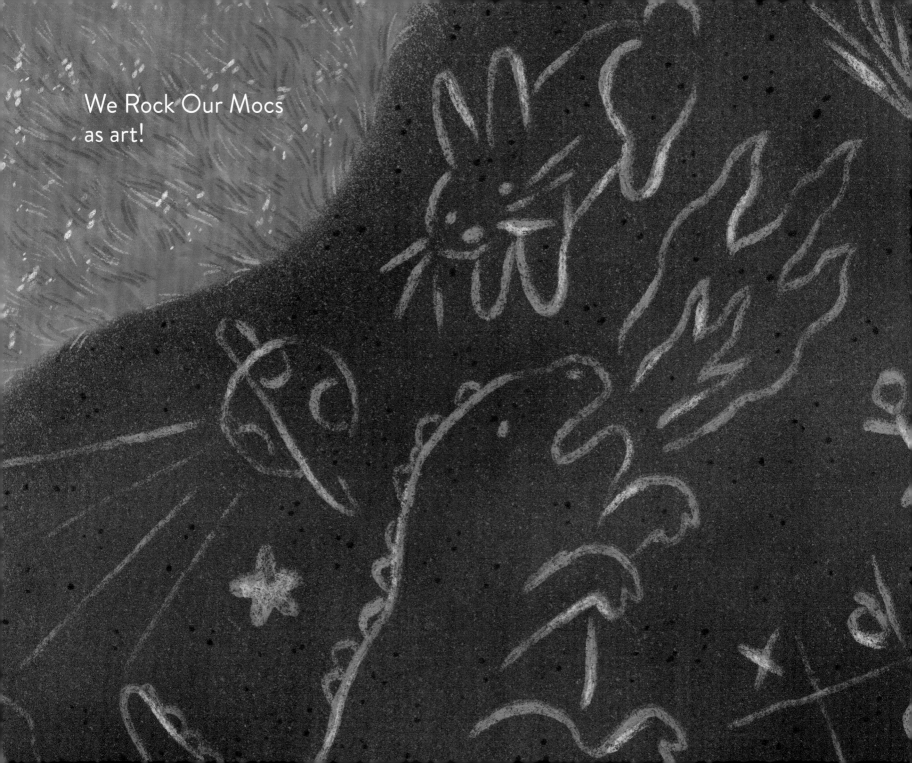

We Rock Our Mocs
as art!

Forrest's Hidatsa mocs
are a blend of colors and shapes.

Maria, who is Osage,
springs up and does
a pirouette.

With memories of our ancestors,
moccasins connect us to our past.
We honor our deep-rooted traditions

ROCK YOUR MOCS DAY!

while adapting to our sacred present
as we Rock Our Mocs!

We Rock Our Mocs
and know our identity!

Standing tall and speaking boldly,
Ajuawak and his classmates
count to ten in Ojibwe.

Ellie leans forward
and listens to Menominee stories.

We Rock Our Mocs
as community!

Tristen from the Seminole tribe
plays tag under the chickees.

Tuscarora twins Kayla and Kylie
wiggle and giggle
as they sing their clan song.

With fringe swaying,
colors flashing,
and soles singing,
we jump higher,
run faster,
and, with our moves,

we are unstoppable.

With beauty on our feet, we love who we are,
and we keep stepping into the future!

We Rock Our Mocs!

Rock Your Mocs Day

Rock Your Mocs Day began in 2011 when Jessica "Jaylyn" Atsye, from Laguna Pueblo, declared that moccasins shouldn't be saved only for ceremonies and powwows. What if Indigenous people could show their Native pride and use them as everyday wear? She chose November 15 during Native American Heritage Month as a day for Native and First Nations people to wear moccasins.

Rock Your Mocs Day steadily grew in popularity when Jessica involved Emergence Productions to spread the celebration across the United States and Canada and around the world. Schoolchildren and adults began to wear their mocs on November 15. Eventually, the organizers selected an entire week in November for Rock Your Mocs events.

In this story, it was impossible to include all 574 federally recognized American Indian tribes in the United States or the 630 First Nation, Inuit, and Métis communities in Canada. Thus, the North American tribes selected represent the following regions: Pacific (Yurok), Alaska and Canada (Inupiaq), Northwest and Canada (Colville), Rocky Mountain (Little Shell Chippewa), Southwest (Navajo), Western (Hopi-Tewa), Great Plains (Hidatsa), Southern Plains (Osage), Midwest and Canada (Ojibwe), Midwest (Menominee), and Eastern (Seminole and Tuscarora).

Moccasins

Moccasins are the traditional footwear of Indigenous Nations and a significant part of tribal culture. Each tribe has a different name in their language for their footwear. *Moccasin* comes from the Algonquian word from the Powhatan language, *makasin*, which means "shoe." Today, all tribes commonly use the term *moccasin*.

If you look at the materials from which moccasins are made, you can identify where the moccasins and the person wearing them originate. The environment determines which materials are used and the design of the shoe. For example, in the subarctic, footwear is made with seal, caribou, and/or moose by covering and sewing around a semicircular insert. Moccasins from the Woodland Nations include a center seam in deer- or elk-hide construction. The Great Plains tribes use deer hide, and their moccasins have a separate leather sole, much like other shoes we wear today.

Moccasin-making is a craft that is passed down from generation to generation. Today, there are moccasin-making classes to continue this art form at colleges, in urban American Indian centers, and in communities. It is a joyful activity to gather as a group and make moccasins as many stories, laughter, and a strong feeling of community, identity, and pride are shared.

Moccasin-making is also a beautiful form of artistic expression. Moccasin makers turn footwear, which is an essential piece of clothing, into a vibrant expression of tribal pride and individual style.

Indigenous Children

Many Indigenous children are intertribal and bi- or tri-cultural. This means they may belong to more than one tribal Nation or may be descendants of cultures originating in Europe, Africa, and Asia. In *Rock Your Mocs*, children are identified with a moccasin from one tribal Nation, but these children may belong to other Nations and cultures as well. Therefore, children in the book have been depicted with a great range of skin tones and hair textures, showing their diverse backgrounds. Some children in the book have names that originate in their Native language. Kyah means "rise of the sun and moon and season of spring" in Yurok; Taktuk means "fog" in Inupiaq; Povi means "flower" in Tewa; and Ajuawak means "crosses the river" in Ojibwe.

In addition to having diverse backgrounds, the Indigenous children represented in this book are from various tribal Nations across Turtle Island, which for Indigenous peoples means the continent now commonly called North America. The turtle is a powerful symbol for many tribes. Some Native and First Nations people live in their Nations, and some live in urban or rural areas away from their Nations. In fact, within the borders of the United States, about 70 percent of Native people now live away from their Nations for various economic, political, and historical reasons. Many Indigenous people within Canada also live outside their tribal homelands.
But no matter where Indigenous people live or what we call ourselves,
we Rock Our Mocs with pride!

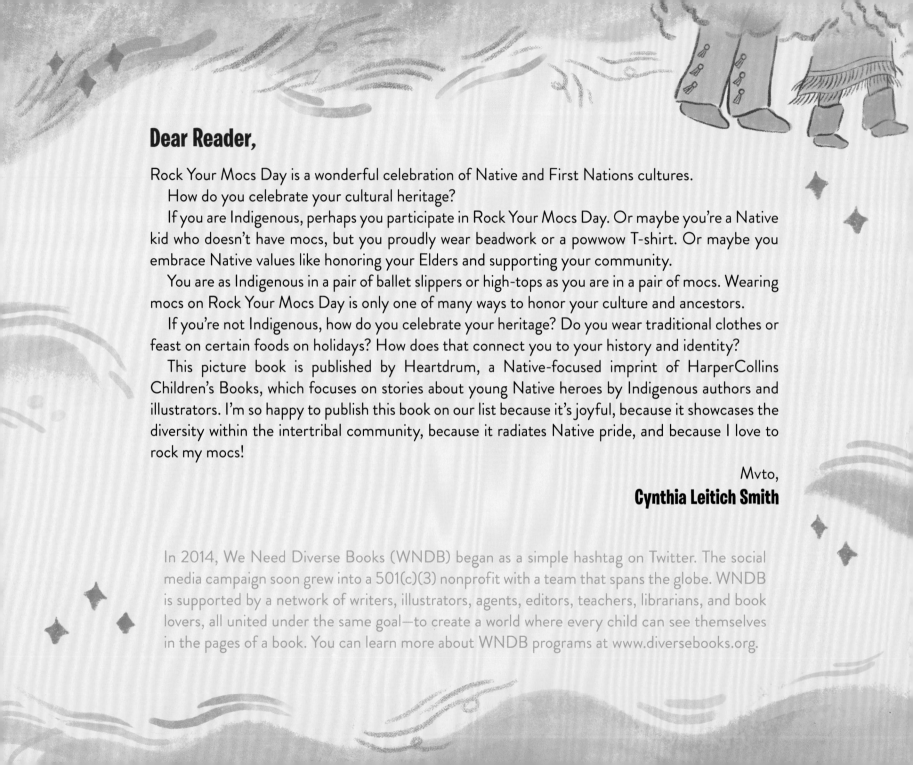

Dear Reader,

Rock Your Mocs Day is a wonderful celebration of Native and First Nations cultures.

How do you celebrate your cultural heritage?

If you are Indigenous, perhaps you participate in Rock Your Mocs Day. Or maybe you're a Native kid who doesn't have mocs, but you proudly wear beadwork or a powwow T-shirt. Or maybe you embrace Native values like honoring your Elders and supporting your community.

You are as Indigenous in a pair of ballet slippers or high-tops as you are in a pair of mocs. Wearing mocs on Rock Your Mocs Day is only one of many ways to honor your culture and ancestors.

If you're not Indigenous, how do you celebrate your heritage? Do you wear traditional clothes or feast on certain foods on holidays? How does that connect you to your history and identity?

This picture book is published by Heartdrum, a Native-focused imprint of HarperCollins Children's Books, which focuses on stories about young Native heroes by Indigenous authors and illustrators. I'm so happy to publish this book on our list because it's joyful, because it showcases the diversity within the intertribal community, because it radiates Native pride, and because I love to rock my mocs!

Mvto,

Cynthia Leitich Smith

In 2014, We Need Diverse Books (WNDB) began as a simple hashtag on Twitter. The social media campaign soon grew into a 501(c)(3) nonprofit with a team that spans the globe. WNDB is supported by a network of writers, illustrators, agents, editors, teachers, librarians, and book lovers, all united under the same goal—to create a world where every child can see themselves in the pages of a book. You can learn more about WNDB programs at www.diversebooks.org.